Our Natural Resources

Audrey Stewart

INFOMAX COMMON CORE READERS

Rosen Classroom™

New York

Published in 2014 by The Rosen Publishing Group, Inc.
29 East 21st Street, New York, NY 10010

Book Design: Mickey Harmon

Photo Credits: Cover, p. 22 (river) straga/Shutterstock.com; pp. 5, 11 mycola/Shutterstock.com; pp. 7, 22 (forests)Valentin Agapov/Shutterstock.com; p. 9 (windmill) Chromatika/Shutterstock.com; p. 9 (oil rig) Zorandim/Shutterstock.com; p. 13 WDG Photo/Shutterstock.com; pp. 15, 22 (rock quarry) vallefrias/Shutterstock.com; p. 17 PhotoStock10/Shutterstock.com; p. 19 Morgan Lane Photography/Shutterstock.com; p. 21 xtrekx/Shutterstock.com; p. 22 (farm) MaxyM/Shutterstock.com.

ISBN: 978-1-4777-2356-2
6-pack ISBN: 978-1-4777-2357-9

Manufactured in the United States of America

CPSIA Compliance Information: Batch #CS13RC: For further information contact Rosen Publishing, New York, New York at 1-800-237-9932.

Contents

America's Resources

Think about the things you use every day. Do you know what they're made of? If you use things made of wood, plastic, glass, or anything else, you're using some of our country's natural resources. America has many natural resources. You can find them in America's rivers, forests, mountains, and farmlands.

From ocean to ocean, America's beautiful land gives us many natural resources.

Why Are Resources Important?

Natural resources are things of value we find in the **environment**. We need them to stay alive, and they give us the things we need and want. Some countries don't have as many resources as America does. So, sometimes we trade our resources with other countries. We're lucky that America has so many resources for us to use!

America's many forests are one kind of natural resource.

To understand what natural resources are, you can **classify** them. We sometimes classify resources based on where they're from or what they're used for. One of the best ways to classify resources is to call them renewable or nonrenewable. Knowing if resources are renewable or nonrenewable helps us use them in the smartest ways.

There are many ways to group resources. This helps us understand what resources are.

Renewable Resources

Some resources are renewable, which means they can be replaced or grown back. Replacing means something new takes the place of what's been used. Some resources do this naturally. Air, water, and sunlight are renewable resources. We don't have to do anything to replace them. That's good, because we need these resources to **survive**.

Almost all living things need water, air, and sunlight to stay alive. These things make our world beautiful, too.

Crops and trees are also renewable resources. After we use them, we can grow new plants to replace them. These resources give us food, **medicine**, clothing, and wood. Wind is also a renewable resource. People have used wind power for a long time. We don't need to replace the wind we use–it just comes back on its own.

People have been using wind power for thousands of years.

Nonrenewable Resources

America also has many nonrenewable resources. Nonrenewable resources can't be replaced or they take a very long time to form again. Sometimes it takes millions of years! When something is nonrenewable, we have to be careful about how much we use. If we use too much too quickly, we can run out.

Rocks are one example of nonrenewable resources.

Fossil fuels are nonrenewable resources. They include coal, oil, and natural gas. Fossil fuels are formed deep inside Earth. This can take millions of years. We use fossil fuels to heat and power our homes. We also use them for gas in our cars. Since fossil fuels are nonrenewable, some people worry we'll run out one day.

It takes a lot of work to get fossil fuels from Earth.

Doing Your Part

Sometimes, we use resources faster than we replace them. One way to **conserve** Earth's resources is by recycling and reusing things we already have. That way, we won't keep using our resources to make new things. We can reduce our use of fossil fuels by riding bikes and turning lights off when we leave the room.

Everyone must do their part to help our environment!

WE
RECYCLE

Can you think of other ways that you use natural resources in your everyday life? Almost everything we use started off as a natural resource. Whether they're renewable or nonrenewable, it's important to think about how much of our resources we use. Using our resources carefully helps Earth stay healthy!

America has many resources, and it's important to take care of them!

Resources Are Everywhere!

America is a big country with many natural resources.
Do you know where to find them?

	Where	Resource	Use
	farms	crops and plants	→ food for people and animals
	forests	trees	→ wood and paper
	lakes and rivers	water	→ needed to stay alive
	Earth	rocks and fossil fuels	→ glass, plastic, metal, and much more

Glossary

classify (KLAH-suh-fy) To arrange in groups or classes.

conserve (kuhn-SUHRV) To save or keep safe.

environment (ihn-VY-ruhn-muhnt) Everything that surrounds us.

medicine (MEH-duh-suhn) A drug people take to treat sickness.

survive (suhr-VYV) To stay alive.

Index